Naughty Pleasures & Desires: Taboo Erotica Volume 3

Erotica - Four Short Stories

Howie Hayes

Copyright © 2014 by Speedy Publishing LLC

All rights reserved. No part of this publication may be reproduced, distributed or transmitted in any form or by any means, including photocopying, recording, or other electronic or mechanical methods, without the prior written permission of the publisher, except in the case of brief quotations embodied in critical reviews and certain other noncommercial uses permitted by copyright law. For permission requests, write to the publisher, addressed "Attention: Permissions Coordinator," at the address below.

Speedy Publishing LLC (c) 2014
40 E. Main St., #1156
Newark, DE 19711
www.speedypublishing.co

Ordering Information:
Quantity sales; Special discounts are available on quantity purchases by corporations, associations, and others. For details, contact the "Special Sales Department" at the address above.

-- 1st edition

Manufactured in the United States of America

WARNING

This book contains sexually explicit scenes and adult language. It may be considered offensive to some readers. This book is for sale to adults ONLY.

* * * * * * * * * * * * * * *

Please store your books wisely where underage readers cannot access them

Table of Contents

Publisher's Notes i

Book 1: Master and Slave 1

Book 2: Lessons from the Hired Help 16

Book 3: Cuckolded by His Boss 31

Book 4: Afraid to Lose Him 46

More Books by Howie Hayes 61

Publisher's Notes

Disclaimer

This publication is intended to provide helpful and informative material. It is not intended to diagnose, treat, cure, or prevent any health problem or condition, nor is intended to replace the advice of a physician. No action should be taken solely on the contents of this book. Always consult your physician or qualified health-care professional on any matters regarding your health and before adopting any suggestions in this book or drawing inferences from it.

The author and publisher specifically disclaim all responsibility for any liability, loss or risk, personal or otherwise, which is incurred as a consequence, directly or indirectly, from the use or application of any contents of this book.

Any and all product names referenced within this book are the trademarks of their respective owners. None of these owners have sponsored, authorized, endorsed, or approved this book.

Always read all information provided by the manufacturers' product labels before using their products. The author and publisher are not responsible for claims made by manufacturers.

Print Edition 2014

BOOK 1: MASTER AND SLAVE

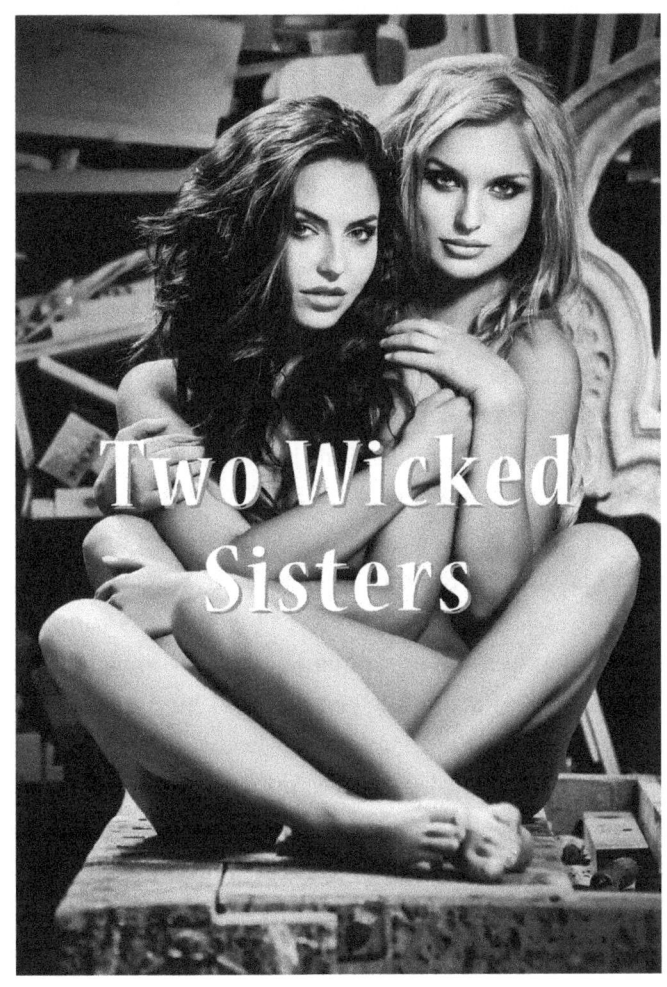

The goosebumps had never left since he had kissed his wife good-bye that morning and the quizzical look on her face had spoken volumes although she had only kissed him back. Now, on his knees and waiting in the prone position, he had no idea what to expect, only that her anger was a terrible thing to see.

When the door opened, he dared not look in her direction, even though the steady click of her heels coming toward him made his heart lurch with every step. In this room, he was a slave, nameless, powerless, but not without a heart. He remembered that every time she touched him.

"Slave," her voice caressed and teased him, like a tongue floating along all the tender places on his skin, something he could picture her doing easily when he was far from her sight. In moments like this, he knew she was far more likely to spit on him than embrace him. "Why do you try to fight it so hard, slave?"

It was a rhetorical question, it was unnecessary to answer and one that only she knew anyway. "Why do you make it so difficult?" she stood by his side now, and a long red fingernail on his chin forced his face up to stare at her. As always, the sight of her took his breath away, her long, black flowing locks running down her back, swinging with every movement of her hips, her pale face with the dark eyes and the full, red lips that he had always longed to kiss. His eyes traveled down her body, her perfect breasts molded under the heavy, leather corset, her slender hips wrapped in more tight leather, the long legs almost entirely concealed by her thigh-high boots, she was a goddess. A wet dream that could easily melt into a nightmare, as he had recently discovered.

"Time for your punishment, slave," she murmured after letting his face go. "Up on your feet," she commanded and he found that his legs trembled so badly that once he was up, he feared that he would fall. Once his wrists and ankles were locked into her shackles, he could strain and pull and wince all he liked, there was no escape until she was done with him.

"Let me put this away for you," her voice was a husky

whisper and when she grabbed his half-hard cock he found himself moaning from her touch, if even for a moment, his affection dripping on her soft palm, he wanted to thrust, but knew before his hips moved that the punishment would outweigh the seconds of pleasure.

She smirked as she grasped him, wrapping a leather strap quickly around the base of his dick which made him fully hard and flail in the device. With more quick movements, her skilled hands had his balls separated and tied, his erection was bound and she held the other end of the strap securely in her hand so that she controlled his penis. The first jerk on his tether was sweet and painful at the same time, as was everything she did. He sighed and bit his lip as the leather bit into his tender skin.

She stepped behind him and the feel of her pulling on his cock and balls, pulling his hard-on back between his legs was excruciating and wonderful and his thighs flexed and his hands grabbed for the chain above his cuff, as if to give himself strength for what would follow.

"This is long overdue, slave," she told him, close to his ear, her breath touching him like fingers wondering down his bare back. "You've been spoiled, haven't you?"

"Yes, Mistress," he panted, knowing that she must be right, she always was.

"Thinking that you could get away with that, pathetic!" her voice was ice and steel and his heart galloped in his chest, harder with every word. "Who do you belong to, slave?"

She yanked hard on his bulging erection so that it was more pain than pleasure this time and he cried out as he quickly answered, "You, Mistress."

"You need to remember that, don't you?" she barked at him, and he could hear the unmistakable sound of the paddle drawing back, the weight of it drawn up in the air, knowing it would come down with a crash on his bottom in a moment.

When she struck, he saw colors and could hardly breathe,

somehow he managed to answer, "Yes, Mistress," while he whimpered. She struck again, it was harder this time and the electric current was a fire running down from his cheek and the back of his thigh. The pain came again and again; he could picture the long, purple welts rising on his bottom that would shout at him every time he looked in the mirror and tried to sit down. She would leave him raw and aching this time.

It continued, he had lost count of how many times the paddle had landed and now she was yanking on the strap that bound his dick, the rough material digging into him, the pressure on his hard cock made him leak down his thigh, hot, sticky and just confirming what she obviously knew; that he belonged entirely to her.

"Are you done trying my patience?" she asked him quietly, the paddle still in mid-air.

"Yes, Mistress, please forgive me," he whined and his voice sounded as pitiful as he felt. What was he thinking that he could walk away? It had been laughable from the beginning.

"Very good," she replied and a barrage of lighter slaps came, the paddle smacking each cheek, striking him on the underneath curve, dangerously close to his tied sack. When he tried to jump out of the path of the stinging leather, she laughed as she pulled his strap hard once more, listening to his plea for mercy.

"You'll remember this, won't you, slave?" she was softness and her voice purred and her breath along his neck made him tremble with desire.

"Yes, Mistress," he wanted to beg her to be gentle, to run her soft fingers down all of his aching places.

"Just so you remember, slave, I'm going to fill you up with my cock now," she was pushing him forward and he stood on his toes and the balls of his feet, his burning bottom upturned now so that she had easy access to his ass. He ached to feel her inside, pushing him to the edge of his pleasure, watching him hang on precariously, unsure if she would be benevolent or laugh wickedly as he fell to his knees, denied.

The first thrust was easy, the head of her wide cock opening him, sliding inside and staying, stretching him for the rest of her meaty shaft. "Do you like that, slave?" she asked, as if she didn't know that it was all he wanted.

"Yes, Mistress," he panted and moved back to take more, feeling her slide in deeper, then deeper again until she was completely inside him, down to the base of the strap-on.

She pumped in and out of him now, his tight, puckered opening was impaled on her cock, she took him slowly and he felt her right hand reach around to the leather strap that still trapped his dripping dick. As she slowly unwrapped him, he felt his erection wagging wildly, the drizzle of precum running down the length of his shaft now. The freedom would be worse now, unable to touch himself, knowing that she completely controlled whether or not he'd be given permission at all, he would simmer and pulse, perhaps for days as he waited.

She fucked him now, a full thrust, withdrawing, another full thrust, her skin pressed into his, he no longer felt or acknowledged the pain of his hot bottom and thought of only her inside him, possessing him the way he had always longed for. "Who do you belong to, slave?" she asked, although they both knew it was entirely unnecessary.

"You, Mistress," he could only whisper it, wishing he could tell her while his face was buried between her breasts.

"I didn't hear you, tell me again," she wouldn't allow him an inch.

"You, Mistress, I belong to you," he wailed and as he worked his hips back and forth to take every inch of her dick, he knew he always had been hers, ever since the first minute he saw her.

"That's a good boy," she panted now and she reached up to unlock his right hand. He was free and he clamped his palm around his dick immediately and tightly, shivering as he touched himself, keeping her time, his hand down around the base when she was fully inside, up toward the wet head when she pulled back. Working his hips to meet her and take her, he was sobbing with want and on the verge of cumming, slowing his hand down, waiting for her permission.

She knew what he wanted and continued fucking him without a word of consent, reaching around and pinching a nipple, the sensation of her touch there riding down the length of him to his cock. "Do you want to cum, slave?" she knew that he wouldn't dare let a drop spill without her allowing it.

"Yes, please Mistress," he held his cock at the base, a trickle of saliva running down his chin.

She brought the full weight of the strap-on down and the pressure against his prostate pushed him over, unable to stop, he clenched tight around his Mistress' cock and rode the current of her hand on him, her erection owning him and he felt the orgasm there, just underneath the surface. "You will be my good slave now, won't you?" she pressed into him with the smallest movement.

"Yes," he was sputtering and could hardly breathe, ready to burst.

"Then you may cum," she finally gave permission and with two more short strokes of his hand, he exploded, wads of his briny, thick climax shot from him, coating his hand, he had clamped down on her enormous dick and moaned as he felt the release continue to travel down every inch of his body, inside and out.

His Mistress slowly withdrew the strap-on and he felt her hands moving about, above to unlock his other hand and below to take off the restraints on his ankles. She would leave him to dress and clean-up but not without the soft touch of her hand running down along his naked back, watching his every muscle quiver. "Be a good boy," she warned him this time, her voice was honey in his ear but he knew what she meant.

"Yes, Mistress," he hung his head, he had learned his lesson.

Without another word, let alone the tender kiss that she would sometimes grace him with, she clicked away and disappeared the same way she had come.

The house was quiet when he arrived, his wife startled him when she walked up behind him and placed her hand on his belly, her soft mouth kissing his neck once. He closed his eyes and felt his face grow hot under her sweet caress. Why did he feel the incessant need to drag himself back to that degradation when she waited for him with open arms.

He turned to face her and greeted her with an open mouth, tasting her full lips, the top and then the bottom before slipping his tongue inside and feeling her warm and wet. He stood back to look at her for a moment, her sheath of brown hair was tied back in a braid, her shoulders were bare in the sundress that she wore and her décolletage seemed to beckon him. Her face was free of make-up, just the way he liked and her smile confirmed that he really didn't need anything, or anyone, else.

"How was your day, honey?" she asked.

"It was fine," he swallowed hard, he hated himself for the incessant lying that had become his life the last months.

"I'm glad, you looked worried this morning," and he realized that his poker face was futile with her, she had known him all these years.

"No, Becca, I'm fine," he smiled and felt the familiar determination well up to never have to feel this shame wash over him again. He was done with her; Rebecca was beautiful, a wonderful, sweet woman and he was lucky to have her. "Do we have time before dinner? I just want to jump in the shower," he had to wash the afternoon off.

"Sure, Michael, it's going to be thirty minutes," she slid one hand into his and her fingers stroked with feather light strokes that made his penis pulse once more. "Oh," she added quickly, "Vicky's coming too."

His stomach lurched when he heard her name. "Do we

have to have her over again?" Michael was determined to keep his voice steady.

"Honey, she's my sister and besides, I think she's lonely," his wife dismissed him with a click of her tongue before walking back to the kitchen.

He trudged up the stairs to the master bath slowly, the weight of the next few hours suddenly felt like he was back in her chains, trying desperately to escape, his muscles shaking from the effort. After he had showered, he stood in front of the mirror and turned his bottom toward the glass and his head, noting how she had marked him, a pattern of dark welts had risen in the hours since he had left her. Running a hand down his backside, every touch was painful, he wouldn't be able to sit or move for the next two days without quickly remembering the heavy strokes, which had been her intention all along.

As he dressed for dinner, he noticed that his hand was shaking. Michael admonished himself, he had to let it go. When he heard the voices of the two women downstairs, a giggle here, a laugh and the happy chatter and sounds of dishes, he looked in the mirror once more, he could do this.

When he saw the two of them sitting at the table though, the panic swept over him once more. She must have heard him approaching and Vicky, her long, black hair swept up in a bun, she was almost unfamiliar in the jeans and tee-shirt, Michael was unaccustomed to her in anything but leather.

"Michael, how was your day?" she asked, he wondered if Becca knew the difference between her smile and her smirk.

"Good," he forced himself to speak without the usual title of Mistress and sat down with a grimace. His punishment would never end.

He was convinced that they were both in on it when Becca told him that she was making up the guest bedroom so that Vicky could spend the night. He studied her face, looking for a sign, a knowing eyebrow, something, but he could find nothing. He was just paranoid, Becca was just lovely in every way and he wallowed in his shame again.

Michael wore pajama bottoms to bed to hide the tell-tale paddle marks across his backside that would announce his predilections; his dick was at half-mast, leaking a trail of want, leaving a pronounced wet spot on the crotch of the material. He groaned when he thought of his sister-in-law down the hall, so close and yet so untouchable, he imagined tip-toeing to Mistress Victoria's room after Becca's gentle breathing became a soft snore, pushing the door open silently and creeping to her side, stealthily sliding between her covers and ravishing her.

Becca came out of the bathroom, her skin was pink from the hot bath, her hair was loose from the braid and tumbled down her small shoulders in waves. She was bare under the white tee-shirt and her nipples were hard peaks that jostled up and down as she walked, her heavy breasts bouncing with no underwire to frame them. He watched the tee-shirt ride up as she crawled across the bed on her knees to get into her favorite position. Naked below as well, Michael caught the glimpse of her small, lower lips and knew that in spite of his panic, all of his secret longings, he couldn't resist making love to her.

"Baby," he opened his arms to her, her head nestling on her favorite spot, she could hear his heart pounding beneath her ear there and sometimes he wondered if she could just tell by listening to it, what a tangled web was inside.

Becca kissed him on the chest and then moved her head to the right and found his own erect nipple, swirling her tongue around it and sucking him softly between her two velvety lips. He was amazed every time, the contrast between the two sisters, Becca sweet, Victoria sharp; Becca's mouth was like warm milk along every inch of him, Victoria could cut him like a knife through soft butter.

He couldn't stop sighing and the sounds of his passion became louder as his wife stroked his erection through the front of his pajamas, then reached inside and slid her fingers from the wet tip of him to the root. "God, yes," he pushed down on the bed and groaned in pain as he felt his hot, throbbing bottom scrape against the sheets. How could he forget, even as Becca stripped down his pants and fondled every inch of him, who had marked him?

Michael saw her take her position between his legs and he couldn't help but wonder if Victoria would ever lie in the prone position to pleasure him like this. It was actually laughable to imagine. He was her toy, her plaything to taunt and twist and fuck, Becca loved him and when he felt her wet tongue slide down the length of him, licking his puddle of precum, tracing her tongue slowly down to swirl and suck on his testicle, one at a time, he renewed his vow to never go back to that woman again.

She slid his penis in her mouth, wrapping her velvet lips around him tightly and rocking her head back and forth to take every inch of him. "Becca," he called out, no longer caring if his Mistress heard him taking his pleasure in the arms of another. "Turn around, my love," he wouldn't even have to beg her, she'd gladly turn and place her hips above his head, her slender hips, her heart-shaped bottom and her creamy thighs spread open so that he could kiss and taste her from her clitoris all the way to her anus.

Michael's tongue touched the tip of her full clit, so erect and clamoring for his attention, he could feel the tingle that ran down her spine as he licked her there. With her wet mouth still tight around him, her tongue bathing him from base to tip, he lapped at her, the way he knew that she craved, easy, slow movements, his tongue sliding softly along and around her pink nub, in a patient rhythm. He reached up to hold her down on his face, as if she would ever move or stop him.

Without looking at Becca's face though, as had always been the case since she had set fire to his life, he flashed back easily to his Mistress and all of the pent-up, fiery fantasies of loving her that he'd had since that first drunken, fumbling night when he'd given her all the ammunition she'd need to break him.

He started to flick his tongue back and forth faster, feeling his wife's clit pulsate and grow with every touch, her sweet juices sliding down her parted lips, dripping on his lips, down his chin, he could feel a puddle of her on his neck. Listening to her purr on his dick while she sucked him harder and harder, Michael imagined that she was Victoria after all, writhing and gyrating on his mouth, using him once again for her pleasure. He wondered if his Mistress would have the cotton-candy sweetness of Becca or something more potent, something that would be intoxicating but poisonous; he imagined that he would never be able to stop drinking until it was too late.

His wife was cumming and he pursed his lips to hold her clitoris between them, the sensation of her clit, pumping and filling his mouth with her delectable, sticky orgasm was suddenly Victoria instead, it was her large, dark clit, fully erect it looked like a small cock protruding from her slender, red lips and he imagined her sitting on his face, grinding herself against him and commanding him to drink, swallow and start again.

Becca released his erection from her mouth and moved gracefully down his body, still facing away from him, she grasped his cock and rubbed the wet slit of him against her still vibrating clitoris, she was erect and it felt like she could enter him that way. "Becca, please," was as close to begging as she would require and she forced his entire hard-on inside in one fast movement of her hips.

She was soaking wet and all he could do was push up to bury himself deep inside while she controlled the rhythm. She was hot silk, tight and perfect, every ridge and crevice of his cock was covered with her cream and he heard himself beg even though it wasn't required, yes and please and my love were the words he called out over and over as Becca fucked him slowly. He watched her shimmy up on his dick and then drive down, the sounds of her moans getting louder and louder with every movement.

Michael closed his eyes and moved his hips with her, but in

his mind's eye, he saw Victoria ride him, in hard, punishing, short strokes, she would take his dick like she gave him hers, completely in control, he imagined she would be white hot inside and clamp around his dick like a vice. When he pictured her bottom bouncing on top of him he bit his lip and clenched to stop himself from cumming. She might not even allow his release at all. Instead she might scoot back up to his face and drown him in her juicy ejaculate that she would command him to suck and swallow until the very last spurt.

Becca called out his name and suddenly Michael returned, his dick was buried in his wife, he could feel her convulse and reached out to push her down by the hips on his erection, feeling her tighten around him, tensing and releasing, covering him with all of her sweet wetness, marking him in a way that her sister never had. With that thought, he couldn't hold back another moment and his cry was loud and echoed in his ears as his climax ripped through him, his cock shuddering with every wave, filling Becca with a flood of his semen.

He could never flash back to Victoria though once Becca had turned around, sliding off his now dick, soft and caked in their joined orgasms now, lying against his thigh, when she was back in his arms and they melted together as only the two of them could, this was when it was as if he'd never fallen, Victoria was just a blur, a mistake that could have happened if he'd let it go that far.

Michael kissed Becca on the top of her head before dozing off, she would stay here in his arms, somehow moving to her own side undetected in the night. He wished that he would wake up with her in the same place. He woke up with a startle, a noise somewhere in his dream became real and he bolted up, off the bed. Becca was curled up in a heap to his right, and he held his breath and reached for her when he heard the creaking noise again. It was the door, he could see it move slowly back and he heard the soft, sliding footsteps back down the hallway. His Mistress, keeping an eye on him.

He lay down without making a sound, fresh goosebumps covered his body from head to toe now as he wondered what would lie in store, what punishment would be exacted after he had just pledged allegiance to the woman that could, on a whim, bring it all crashing down.

Michael hadn't been back to see her all week. He told himself it was like going to rehab, there would be good moments, where he felt clean and good, as if he could hold his head up high once more and meet Becca's gaze. There would be horrible moments that seemed to drag on all day and dig into his skin like her fingernail sinking into his throbbing nipple. He could almost taste her then and his hand would shake as he went to grab the phone and poke her name with his index finger and start the process all over again. He put his cell phone in a drawer so that it would take him longer, trying not to fall back into her clutches.

He woke up that morning with a hard-on that lurched and quivered for immediate attention, the memory of her skewering him, opening up his virgin hole and claiming her stake as she fucked him hard and slow. He had fought it so hard the first time, he had clenched his cheeks as well as his teeth together, determined to fight and in moments he had opened and was sobbing like a freshly deflowered teenage girl, backing up into her and hoping she'd never stop. He needed to feel her inside him again.

Michael went to the drawer where he had tucked a dildo about the same size as her cock that she would wear while she paddled him mercilessly. Becca would be out for her morning run, he could take it in the shower, lube himself up, and work the large cock in and out of his hungry ass while he pictured her making him his bitch one more time.

It wasn't there. His heart was flipping non-stop in his chest, little fingers of fire reached out of his ribcage and he felt the fear and desperation claw at him. What if he had been found out? What if he couldn't fulfill his nasty need? He knew he'd be on his knees in hours no matter what mental games he attempted to play on himself.

"Looking for something?" the voice was like a sharp, metal edge. When he whirled around, everything he had feared for the last months was suddenly real, palpable. His wife was holding the thick, black cock between two fingers, waving it back and forth as if he were a dog and she were going to make him beg for a treat.

"How'd you know?" he gulped, realizing as soon as he asked that he was already revealing too much with just the question.

"Michael, really?" she smirked and suddenly she was a mirror image of her sister, mocking him, tempting him, she was dressed only in black, sheer panties and a matching bra, and he remembered his dripping dick as he took in all of her. "You really didn't think I knew all along?"

"I'm sorry," he looked to the floor and wondered if groveling would be enough for the other woman in his life.

"I told her the first night, slave," Victoria strode through the door, clad in leather from head to toe, smelling of her musky perfume and sex and all the things he didn't dare let himself think of let alone say. "Why are you standing?" she snarled at him and his reflexes came back quickly as he slipped back into the supplicant's position that she required. "That's better," she told him as she walked closer to her sister, the two voices were low and he guessed that the chatter he always had dismissed between them had been far more important than he ever guessed.

"Today, slave, you'll show Mistress Becca how well trained you are," his wicked Mistress declared, "up on the bed, on your knees," she prompted, snapping her fingers to show how quickly she wanted him to respond.

Yes, like a dog, he realized that this would ultimately lead to him groveling to both women, humiliating himself again and yet again. He couldn't deny that he deserved it but it was no less shameful.

Becca moved to the head of the bed, a strap-on cinched

around her small hips, his long, heavy dildo now locked in place and she touched his lips with the head, circling his mouth, dragging the thick dick across his upper lip and then his lower, looking to see how wet he'd made her. "I hear that you love to suck cock for your Mistress, slave. Is that true?" she asked him in the honey tone that he was used to hearing and he shook his head yes.

His wife slapped his face hard enough that tears came to his eyes, her voice hardened when she spoke, "You will address me as Mistress, slave. Do you love to suck cock, yes or no?"

"Yes, Mistress," he whined, his face was now hot from the sting as well as his shame.

"Then today you will me how well you've been trained, slave," she informed him and added, "open your mouth."

He felt his wife force the dick to the top of his throat, he almost wretched, unused to the length of the dick between his lips. When he saw her slide out and then slide back, her hips pumping and thrusting the cock in and out of him, fucking his face, his own much smaller cock responded, waving wildly, slapping his stomach and leaving a wet trail of his passion to trickle down his pelvis.

Victoria was behind him and he shivered with delight as she forced him open to take her cock in his puckered hole. Yes, he would be used and violated by both of them again and again and he deserved nothing less. The images in his mind, both of them, taking turns with their play thing, took his breath away and he almost couldn't contain his happiness.

BOOK 2: LESSONS FROM THE HIRED HELP

He was used to snapping his fingers and getting what he wanted, it had been that way his whole life. Edward didn't even have to bark or shout or dole out commands, one eyebrow raised on his forehead was more than enough for his personal assistant to know that something wasn't satisfactory.

He couldn't imagine why his wife was being so difficult lately. Marla was a goddess, but suddenly it seemed to have gone to her head. Tall, built like a lingerie model, her long, black hair and her creamy, white skin and her emerald, green eyes had opened many doors for her. Even she had to see that marrying him had given her something far better than anything else she could have dreamed of before. How could she be so damn ungrateful?

Edward had come home late on purpose this evening, more drinks at the club than he should have had, he was barely able to take the stairs and drag himself to their bed. As he stood, he held on to the wall and then the chair as he undressed and slipped as quietly as possible under the sheets to take his place at her side.

He glanced over at her, her full lips were slightly parted and even though he was feeling resentful, it didn't take away his desire to kiss her. He crept closer and he could feel her breath on his cheek, he felt himself stirring between his legs and thought of waking her. He was too drunk to last, but she would be accommodating.

Edward pulled the sheet down from her neck and discovered that Marla was naked, her usual big, baggy tee-shirt that she wore to bed was gone and every delectable curve was naked and just inches away. As she breathed, her full, round breasts moved and seemed to beckon him. He looked further down and saw that her right leg was bent and the position left her pink, bare lips free to be touched and fondled. He let out a low groan, almost wishing now that he'd skipped the cocktails and made his way home sooner.

On the other side of her slender thigh, he felt something hard on the sheet next to her. Something a foot long and solid, cylindrical, and he grabbed it. Rolling over and holding it up in the light from the window, there was no mistaking it, but he couldn't help but feel shocked. A huge, pink dildo, still sticky and smelling of his wife's juicy cunt, he imagined that after masturbating with it, she had fallen asleep, exhausted from the orgasm she'd had all over it.

He was embarrassed that he was holding it and then even more embarrassed that he was smelling it, holding the end of the pink, rubber up to his nose and inhaling her essence that had been left behind. Edward's dick quivered and he felt the first, few wet drops of his want dribble on his pelvis. He wanted to be angry, in fact, he was, what was so lacking that she needed to fuck herself with something so much larger than him.

It was that thought that made his hard-on urgent and he stopped thinking about anything else but the image of her, spread-eagle on the bed, her perfectly manicured fingers fondling her nipples while she fed herself the biggest cock he'd ever seen. He closed his eyes and gripped his dick hard, stroking up and down as he watched her in his mind's eye work the huge dildo in slowly, seeing her lips spread wide, dripping with her sweetness.

Edward didn't realize what he was doing until the tip of the cock she had cum all over was in his mouth, and once it was there, there was no turning back. He licked it, ran his tongue over the huge, solid head and tasted her cream in his mouth. He jerked himself harder and faster then, watching her take the big dick further and further inside, her hips thrusting and riding it, her pouty mouth open wide with her screams of ecstasy. She came in long waves, with the dildo buried all the way to the base inside and he felt himself let go as he pictured it. Sucking on the tip of the used cock, his orgasm was sudden and left his whole body shaking.

Once he felt the last spasm dash against his belly, he looked at the cock in his hand, still touching his lips and threw it on the bed in disgust. After he'd washed up and got back into bed, he blamed it quickly on the alcohol and rolling over, far away from the little whore, and fell asleep.

Marla was never awake before him, the little princess always slept in and yet, when Edward's hand reached out to touch her side of the bed this morning, he found it empty. He panicked, could he have slept late? A quick glance at the alarm clock told him that it was only six.

After checking the bedroom and the master bath, there was no sign of her, she wasn't in the kitchen and why would she be, she never cooked. He poured a cup of coffee and walked out on the expansive deck, noticing the first rays of sun in the east and then, his wife's long, black hair off in the distance. She came closer and her face came into view, she wasn't alone. The man next to her towered over her, as tall as she was, Edward could see that he was broad, wide across the chest and his chocolate colored skin gleamed. As they came closer, Edward could see her laugh, tossing her locks and touching his hand.

His face was hot and he felt the vein throb at his temple by the time they noticed that he was watching them.

"Good morning, my love," Marla seemed to know that she was far too close to the man and moved away quickly as she waved.

"Would you like to explain yourself?" he refused to acknowledge the taller man but saw out of the corner of his eye that he was smiling, showing his perfect, pearly white teeth.

"Oh, Edward, this is Emmanuel," she touched the big, black man's chest for just a moment and it was far too long for Edward, "he's going to be putting in the gazebo. We were just talking about it."

"Nice to meet you," Edward was determined to act casually and headed toward the giant with his right hand outstretched. He shook Edward's hand with his dark, brown paw and never stopped smiling.

The two continued on their walk and Edward went back inside, fuming to himself and putting together a plan to fire Emmanuel at the first opportunity.

He was still contemplating the details when he arrived home that evening. Sober and irritated, still carrying the memory of the shameful masturbation fantasy from the night before, it was his intention to lay down the law with Marla. Just because she was used to batting her eyelashes and shaking her heart-shaped bottom and watching everyone bow down to scrape before didn't mean that the little bitch didn't need to be kept in check. Who did she think she was? He paid for her lifestyle, she owed him some respect.

He was rehearsing it line by line as he made his way upstairs to the bedroom. Upon opening the door, it was all forgotten quickly as she greeted him in black, satin lingerie.

"How's my love tonight?" she asked in the breathy voice that she sometimes used to get her way.

Twirling a piece of her long hair around one index finger, she beckoned to him with the other and he dropped the briefcase and kicked off his shoes before jumping on the bed.

"Edward," she got on top of him, the black lace was see-through and he could see every inch of her lovely breasts and every bit of her bottom through the filmy material. "Did you have a hard day, darling?" she asked him as she ran her hands down his chest.

"Yes, exhausting," he spoke quietly, lost in the sight of her. Maybe he was being too hard on Marla, she was, after all, breathtaking.

"You work too hard," she cooed and she slowly untied the tie that had been choking him all day, unbuttoned the shirt, shimmied her hips up a bit so that she could grab his belt and free him from the pants that were trapping his throbbing dick inside. He was naked in a few moments and she looked at him with lust in her eyes as she ran a finger down his leaking erection. "Someone's horny."

"Oh, Marla," he sighed and gave up, he couldn't stay mad at her, not when she was licking her lips and about to go down on him.

Her round, wet lips opened and she kissed the head of his dick, he watched the strand of his juice on her upper lip, glistening, and he felt another dribble run down his dick when she licked her lip clean. Marla wrapped her lips around the head of his cock and teased him with the tip of her tongue on his slit and then around the ridge under his tip, then sliding down on his shaft, she swallowed his erection all the way to the bottom.

Edward's heart thudded harder and harder in his chest as he watched her bob up and down on him. Cupping his balls with one hand, she fondled him and reached behind his ball sack with two fingers, gently scraping along the delicate skin of his perineum. Her tongue circled and teased and tasted every inch and he could feel the pleasure of her mouth run all the way down to his toes.

"Jesus," he was panting and moving his hips up to meet her velvety embrace, thrusting into her mouth and down and back in harder, she held him tightly between her soft lips and bathed his shaft. "I'm going to cum," he hadn't planned on it ending so quickly but she had pushed him far past the point of no return and she didn't take her mouth off, only quickened her tempo.

He spurt hard, into her throat and then coated her tongue, he could hear her swallowing his white, salty load and then when she moved up, one little spasm dripped off her bottom lip and onto her chin. She went back down to suck the last spurt directly from inside him.

When she was finished she lay next to him, her hand on his chest, feeling his hard pants bursting from him. Edward rolled toward her and kissed her hand, "I'm sorry darling, I didn't do anything for you," he realized that he hadn't even stripped off the black teddy.

She wiped the last of his semen on the bed beneath her and reached over his head, opened the nightstand drawer and produced the same enormous, pink dildo that she had fallen asleep with last night, the same one he had sucked on. His face was hot as he recalled it. "I can take care of myself," she giggled and holding the dildo in one hand, she reached down to unsnap the material between her legs and revealed her luscious nakedness. "Or you can use it on me?" she was asking him to participate and he didn't know if he was angry or turned on.

"When did you get that?" he asked, pretending it was the first time he'd seen it.

"A little while ago," she smiled and fluttered her eyelashes at him, "do you want to fuck me with this?"

"Sure, I guess," he swallowed, trying to sound as if he wasn't enthused, wondering if he would get another erection if he watched and what it meant if he did. He held the toy in his hand and lay between her legs, seeing how soaked she was, her bare lips were always such an incredible turn-on, something prepubescent and forbidden about it and now her clit was as hard as a stone and pulsing.

The anger came back though as he watched her and thought about it. Marla was far more eager for the toy than she ever was for him. "Why do you need this when you have me?" he asked, not meaning to sound so whiny but it was too late to take it back.

She looked down at him with the huge, green eyes and her face was serious, although her cheeks were still flushed, her face looked as horny as her dripping cunt. "I don't have you tonight, do I?" she raised her eyebrow as if to remind him that he'd already had his fun.

Edward threw down the toy and sat up, "That's different," and he didn't realize that he was confessing until he was half-way done, "but last night, when I came home, I found this in the bed next to you! What are you, some kind of a whore that suddenly can't get enough cock?"

She grabbed the huge, pink toy out of his hand and threw it in the drawer, snapping up the lingerie once more and sat up with a furious look, staring at him through narrowed eyes, she was still sexy even when she was mad.

"I'm not a whore!" she spat the words back at him, "it's not my fault that you can't make me cum," she clamped her hand over her mouth as soon as she said it, but it was too late.

"Maybe if you weren't such a slut, I could," he could barely look at her right now, the anger was coursing through his body.

Marla got off the bed, pulled her thick, cotton bathrobe down from a hook and wrapped it around herself tightly. She looked back, her eyes were hard as glass and she muttered, "Fine, Edward, you get what you deserve then," before storming out and slamming the door behind her.

They hadn't spoken all day, he hadn't seen her before leaving for work and he had checked periodically to see if she had texted him a sweet nothing and an apology. It wasn't like her to stay angry and by the time he arrived home from work, he wondered if she would even be there.

As he walked into the bedroom, he felt the grip on his shoulder without seeing a face. He was being walked across the room, now two giant hands with vice-like strength were holding him in place. He tried to turn around, but it was hopeless. Marla was naked on the bed and her smile could only be described as evil.

"Edward, this is going to be so fun," she giggled and her perfect breasts moved and she drew up one leg so that her pussy was exposed, "well, at least for me it will be."

"What's going on?" he stammered and kept trying to turn, when he looked down he saw the long, wide feet of someone else behind him.

She stood up slowly, all of her succulent curves bouncing as she stepped toward him, stopping to look at him with a smirk and one hand on her hip. "What's going on is that I have had enough of your bullshit," her voice was like a knife in his heart, "you're a terrible lover and you don't even care. Your tiny, little penis is bad enough but now you won't even try to get me off!" Edward was even more humiliated knowing that whoever was holding him now knew everything. "So I've had to get my dick from other places!"

He felt his stomach lurch, "I knew it!"

Marla took two steps closer and poked his crotch with her long nail, "Who could you satisfy with that Edward? Well, now it doesn't even matter, because you don't get to use that anymore."

The hands pulled him around and started dragging him to the corner of the room toward a large cage that he had never seen before. When he looked up, he saw Emanuel's face attached to the huge, brown frame and he shouted, "See, I knew you were fucking this guy!"

Emanuel opened the door to the cage and bent him down, kicking and screaming and pushed him inside, closing the door behind him before Edward could even turn around.

"How could I not fuck him?" she was purring again, and as Emanuel approached, she touched his muscled chest with one hand as she had when she introduced them, running her palm down the sculpted abs. "But now you get a special treat, Edward. Something that all husbands who can't satisfy their wives should get."

"What are you doing?" Edward whimpered.

"I'm going to fuck him and now, you get to watch and see how a real man gets it done," with that she took his hand and led the giant to the marital bed where he grabbed her by arms and kissed her pouty lips tight, first with his lips closed and then gradually opening his mouth and sliding his wide, pink tongue out to lick her upper lip and then invade her mouth. Edward heard the sighs that escaped from her as they kissed deeper and he could see the movements of their tongues touching, tasting back in forth in his wife's mouth. He let out a low, forlorn noise that seemed to describe the pain in his heart as he watched the man pull down the shorts he was wearing and free the cock that had been trapped there. His dick was enormous and slapped his abs when it was unleashed and Edward realized that it was even larger than the pink toy that he'd been so intimidated by.

Angry again, he almost growled when he yelled, "Fucking slut!"

She didn't stop kissing, it was as if he weren't even there and he watched as Marla's hand slowly traveled down the length of his body and found the bulging dick that waited for her. When she broke the kiss, she looked in Edward's direction for one minute to laugh, "You're here to learn, not talk."

Emanuel moved down her perfect body and applied his lips and tongue to every bit, every curve, every crevice, he licked along the bottom of both breasts and then up to her nipples, grazing them softly with his teeth, kissing the side of her belly and working his way down to her hips. All the while, Marla was moaning and her legs were opening wider and wider for him, Edward could see how wet she was from his cage. He held onto the bars and shook them in frustration a moment before Emanuel took his place between her long legs.

The man's wide tongue covered her lower lips when he stroked her with it. Marla cried in delight and Edward could see her cheeks flush and her beautiful mouth open. Edward felt the twinge in his pants and he hated himself for it, but it was undeniable, he was getting an erection while another man pleasured his wife.

Emanuel started to flick his tongue back and forth along the tip of Marla's clit and the wet noises of his mouth matched the movements of Edward's dick in his pants, there was a soaking wet spot on the crotch now and he started rubbing his aching shaft up and down over the damp material while he listened to his wife's first orgasm.

Marla had grasped the man's head and was pushing her hips up to rub herself against his face and Emanuel kept lapping at her faster and faster, sucking down every drop of her creamy orgasm. Edward watched as Marla sank back down to the mattress, the man hadn't stopped kissing her pink pussy and then slowly pushed two of his thick, brown fingers inside her sloppy cunt.

Keeping his mouth on her and fucking her in and out, Edward moaned as he heard them, Marla whispering yes over and over again and the man's lips now sucking on her, her large, erect clitoris was in his mouth and Edward imagined the big pink tongue flitting around and over her, in an irresistible rhythm.

Marla's breath was coming faster and faster as he saw the man sucker harder, the big head was moving up and down as he gave his wife head. When she moaned and screamed, "God, yes, I'm going to cum for you baby," Edward felt the trickle of precum run down into his underwear at the same time that the tremor of sick jealousy ran down his spine.

She squirted, the man had pulled his mouth off to watch as a dollop of her sweet ejaculate shot from her. Edward was mesmerized, it was something that she had never done for him, admittedly, he had never tried or known how, and here she was dousing the lover with hot spasms of her cream. Edward slid his zipper down and yanked out his dick. The shame couldn't possibly be as great as his desire for her right now.

Emanuel buried his face back down in her shivering snatch, kissing, licking, cleaning her and when he looked up at her, murmured, "I love when you cum on my face," before returning to his place and ravishing her some more.

Marla could breathe once more and she looked down at him, her hand between her legs to touch his face, she asked, "come up here?"

With a deep sigh, the big man moved up on the pillow to lie next to her and share her scented orgasm with her, their kisses were even hotter and Edward saw Marla sucking the drippings that had splattered on his lips and he imagined that it was him, there in her arms, making her cum like that, but knew that it never would be.

"It's my turn, baby," she sat up and moved to Emanuel's side, returning the tongue bath that he had given her, her puckered lips open and her pink tongue traced along his chocolate skin, she caressed his huge biceps and ran her mouth down his collar bones, to his chest, pausing to suck on each nipple before licking along his lined abs. When she reached his hard pole, Edward wondered how her mouth could stretch wide enough to take it inside. She didn't give him long to ponder it.

Edward saw Marla's tongue slither slowly around the enormous head and lick her lover, his puddle of precum dripped off the tip of her tongue and she sucked it back in before she nibbled around his deep ridge and grabbed his dick at the base, far too much for her hand to hold, she pulled him into her mouth and Edward cried out when she slowly slid her head down to take him, deeper and deeper inside.

He stroked himself back and forth while Marla sucked the thudding erection, he was amazed at how wide her cheeks were spread and how frothy his shaft was from the saliva in her mouth, she was soaking him and in a few more motions, she would have his dick all the way inside. When Edward thought that the head must be in her throat now, he almost came but took his hand off and merely panted with his mouth open as he watched her work.

She was taking his whole shaft inside now and moving her head back and forth faster and then faster again and Edward jerked himself to the rhythm of his wife pleasuring her lover. The huge, brown dick, the biggest cock he'd ever seen, was so thick and so full of the man's cum, Edward wondered how she'd be able to swallow the buckets of pearly, white ejaculate that would spew from him if she kept up this furious pace.

He shivered and watched her continue, the man reached down, pleading, "Stop, Marla, please, I want to be inside you." Edward felt the shame lurch up inside him again, her lover was far more considerate and would wait until he'd fucked her to spill his release.

She took her mouth off slowly, her tongue teasing him one last time before she moved onto her back, eager to feel his shaft impale her. "God, yes, I can't wait for your huge cock inside me. It's all I can think about," her voice was hoarse with want and Edward started to stroke himself again as he heard her confession. She had been wishing for the lover's cock in her mouth last night and of course, the toy was so that she could imagine Emanuel driving in and out of her; the superior lover had usurped his place.

Her lover got on top of her and his soft, wet kisses started again while he took his dick in his hand and moved the head slowly around her opening, dousing himself with her cunt juices. Marla was moaning before he was even inside and Edward didn't know how much longer he could hold back his own orgasm.

Emanuel had to enter her slowly, just the head slid inside and Marla gasped. Then another inch or two, pulling her lips apart wide to accommodate his girth, her thighs were quivering from the ecstasy his huge dick filled her with. Slowly he continued to push forward until every bit of his engorged erection was deep inside Marla, balls deep in his wife, Edward jerked his tiny cock faster and faster as the man began to thrust.

He pulled all the way out and slammed into her hard, Marla's head moved on the pillow and the scream that came from her was something she had never managed for Edward. He fucked her slow and deep and drove in and out of her, his cock covered in her cream and his heavy balls slapping her with every push. Marla had moved her feet and had her legs wrapped around his ass, Edward watched as the lover reached down to raise her hips and pull her even further down on his shuddering cock.

Edward felt his dick lunge in his hand and he came harder than he ever remembered cumming before, ropes of hot semen shot out of his dick, onto his pants, on his shirt and pooled in his hand. The shame of knowing that his release had been that potent as he watched another man take his wife as palpable but his heart beat so loudly in his ears that he couldn't hear the words that screamed in his brain.

Marla was about to have her own orgasm and told the lover over and over and grasped his head to kiss him and cry into his mouth as she squeezed and held him tight to wash every inch of him with the climax that rocked her. Edward could almost see her snatch grabbing the dick tight and holding him inside, the lover had slowed down his thrust to enjoy the vibration that covered him and his kisses continued.

Emanuel pumped in and out of her with a few even deeper thrusts and with a roar, he exploded deep inside the gorgeous woman on the bed. Edward could see the muscles in his ass flex as he continued to move, burying ropes of sticky cum at the bottom of his wife's soaked pussy. Edward imagined her walking across the room to him, all of his hot saltiness running down her inner thighs and standing before him while he was in the cage. When the thought came to him, he was horrified, but there was no way of stopping the image in his mind of him bending in reverence and licking the alpha male's semen from her. The thought was not going to go away and the shame he had when his dick leaked and moved as he imagined it wouldn't leave either.

Edward wasn't given the opportunity to indulge because the lovers left the bed after a long time of kissing and sighing, walking with the big, brown man's hands around her small waist, they took a shower together and Edward was suddenly sad, alone and unable to watch them.

When they emerged, Marla kissed the lover good-bye and the giant left her in her thick robe, her wet hair lay down her back and the look of contentment on her face was unmistakable. Without speaking to him, she opened his cage and walked to the bed to take her place on the bed.

Edward knew that the sheets would be soaked from their orgasms and wondered how he could sleep in it, but he would. He undressed quietly and lay beside her, waiting for a few minutes before reaching his hand out to hold hers.

"Did you learn anything tonight, Edward?" she asked him, no malice in her voice, she was just soft and tender.

"Yes, Marla," he whispered, coming closer so that he could smell her. "I'm a terrible lover and you deserve so much more." He didn't know if he could ask, his lip trembled and he swallowed hard, deciding to beg her if she needed it. "I have a request, though."

"What is that?" she smiled at him with the full, pouty lips.

"Next time, I'd like to clean you up," he could only mumble it.

"Clean me up in the shower?" she had turned to him so that she could look him in the eye.

Edward touched her face softly and traced his finger along the edge of her round lips that had been kissed so well and so frequently by the lover. "No, I'd like to clean up your lover's cum when he's done."

Marla understood and a low noise escaped her as she cuddled in his arms. Edward would be the second man she'd kiss tonight but there was no denying her, her tongue tasted sweet in his mouth and her breath on his lips gave him goosebumps. "Yes, my love, that would be wonderful," she murmured in his ear before returning to his mouth.

The scene was already playing in his imagination and he broke the kiss to say, "Yes it will be."

Book 3: Cuckolded by His Boss

The bastard was going to make him work late and he hated him even more right now if that was possible. Anthony called his wife to tell her the bad news, "I'm going to be late again," his voice shook with his fury.

"Why is he doing this to you, honey?" Susan asked, her sweet voice was like a kiss in his ear.

"Because he knows I want that promotion," there was a little more to it than that but that was all he would say for now, "he's got me by the balls."

"Well, I'll miss you," her whisper was hot and it made him instantly remember what they were supposed to have been doing tonight, "although I might have to take care of myself."

He groaned, picturing her on the bed, blond hair fanned out on the pillow beneath her and her scrumptious body on display while she touched herself, cheeks flushed, full, pink lips parted and he was instantly hard as a rock, "can you wait for me, Susan?" he would work like a fiend to be a part of that.

"I'll try," she told him in a sing-song voice, meant to tease but all she did was egg him on at this point.

"Let me get going," he told her good-bye and shook his head to rid himself of the slow, sensual images of her and her fingers and the panting noises she made when she came. The slave driver was insatiable and he had no time for daydreams.

Anthony had lost track of time when he heard the knock on his door, "hey, Tony, how's it going in here?" his boss only knocked as a courtesy, he was coming in regardless.

"Hey, great," Anthony looked Charles up and down, five years his junior, the man was an enigma, an annoying combination of everything he hated and wished to be and it killed him to call him "sir". Charles crossed the floor to stand a foot away, tall, dark-haired, he worked out and it showed, he had none of the middle-aged pudge that clung to Anthony, he looked like a well-muscled, sleek predator and that was exactly how he walked.

"So you'll have that finished before you leave tonight?"

Charles was running his hands over things on his desk, as if he owned every personal item as well as Anthony himself. His pulse hammered in his ears and he narrowed his eyes at the man.

"Yes, sir," somehow his voice was polite in spite of his feelings.

"Great," his boss trailed off, his fingers were on the picture frame, a picture of Susan inside, "Jesus, who is this?" the man picked up her picture and ran his hands down it, as if touching her right in front of him.

"That's my wife," Anthony bit his lip and fought the urge to snatch it out of his hands, "we've been married for ten years, sir," he wanted to add, you dumb fuck, you've met her at least ten times, but just smiled instead.

"You're a lucky man," Charles sighed and put the picture back, still staring at her with a lascivious eye, "she is gorgeous."

"Thank you sir," he wanted to scream, "I better get back to work," he shrugged his shoulders as if to dismiss the man.

"You know," Charles had reached out and his powerful hand dug into Anthony's shoulder, squeezing him there, it was quite painful and an unnecessary show of strength, "if I had more employees like you, I'd have a lot less headaches."

His boss left and Anthony rubbed his shoulder, muttering under his breath, if he had more employees, because they belonged to him of course, as if he were actually a slave. He vowed to update his resume this weekend so he could be one step closer to telling the bastard that he quit.

Susan had waited for him and when he drug himself up the stairs, loosening his tie and unbuttoning his collar, he wondered where he would get the energy to fulfill his end of the bargain. Even after pushing open the bedroom door and seeing her there, sitting on the bed, wearing the tiny schoolgirl skirt and the little, white blouse, tied at the waist, the ruffled socks and the stripper heels, his cock fluttered and dripped but he didn't know how long it would last.

"Baby," he rushed to her, throwing the briefcase on the floor, arms open to embrace her, "God, you look amazing," she was even wearing her hair in pigtails as he had suggested.

Susan was a natural flirt and crossed her legs, the bottom half of her ass cheek showing when she did, the tip of her index finger in her mouth, she cocked her head and then took the finger out and blew him a kiss, "thank you."

Anthony undressed quickly and approached her with his hand wrapped tight around the base of his hard dick, moaning as he touched the wet tip of in on her bare leg, back and forth, he wet her thigh and he already knew that he wouldn't last long. "What did you do, baby?" he wanted every dirty, little detail even if he did wind up cumming on her skirt.

"I made a video," she talked to him in her naughty, little girl voice and Anthony started moving his hand up and down on his flailing cock as he listened. "I wore this outfit, just like you wanted, and I made a video of me touching myself all over."

"God, that's hot," he whimpered, "did you have the little, white panties on?"

"Of course," she grinned and showed him her tiny, white thong that barely left anything to the imagination, "and then I posted the video."

The thought of strange men, horny and drooling all over themselves as they watched his hot wife run her dainty fingers over her bare, wet snatch was a fantasy that he could not rid himself of. They had spoken of it while in bed for over a year and she had finally agreed to make it real.

"And what happened? Did you get a lot of responses?" of course she had, he just needed to hear the words as he hovered close to his orgasm.

"My God, I got so many of them, all kinds of perverts," she giggled and that just made it even sexier, "but one of them is really interested and kind of sexy too."

Her eyebrows went up when she told him and he clenched

his teeth, trying to hold back his climax, he wanted to hear her talk about the man that made those innocent, white panties wet and cling to her sweet slit. "What did he say?" Anthony was panting as he jerked and shuddered.

"He said he wanted to watch me some more, wanted to watch me taking a big dildo before he came over, so that he knew I'd be ready for his huge cock," her fingers trailed down to her legs and when she writhed and pulled up the skirt, he stopped masturbating for a moment just to hold on a few seconds more. "He said that he can hardly wait to fuck me with it while you watch," her fingers slipped over the top of the panties and she started rubbing her clit while he stared and sputtered.

"Susan, yeah, tell me how much you're going to like fucking that dick, tell me baby," he begged her, about to unload spurts of semen on her leg.

She purred and wiggled her finger faster as she told him, "I can hardly wait to bend over the bed while he rams that enormous cock in me, with you sitting right here," she patted the bed, "you have to watch me with a real man, don't you, baby?"

She knew what he needed by now and he shouted as the first hard explosion ripped from him and he spasmed, a long line of his cream hit her leg, then her skirt, wrecked her little panties and coated her belly. Anthony put his hand out to the mattress to prop himself his legs were shaking so badly.

"See, I know what you want," she murmured as she pulled her moist fingers from her ruined underwear and held them out for him to clean with his tongue before opening her arms to hold him tight.

Before he drifted off, he told her about his awful day with Charles and his visit to the office, "God, I hate that guy," he shut his eyes, one arm under her pillow.

"Poor Anthony," she patted his chest like he was a small child, "he's probably just jealous of you."

It was Saturday night and they had a date. Unlike their

typical date night, this would involve a third party and as Anthony finished getting ready, he realized that he was more nervous than he'd been for their first date. All he knew about the man was what Susan had told him, which he was tall and looked to be in good shape; Anthony patted his gut and wished that he were thinner.

He frowned at himself, this is what he had begged her for, it wasn't time to succumb to his insecurities. It was just taking the fantasy to the logical conclusion.

Susan looked amazing and he felt his heart hammering as he stared at her coming down the hall. The tight, short black dress that she wore skimmed every curve; it stopped maybe three inches below her round, heart-shaped bottom. Her heels set it off and her long, blond hair was scooped up at the back, tendrils skimming her cheeks, pink lipstick gleamed on her full mouth, she was taking it even more seriously than he had imagined.

"Hey, beautiful," Anthony grabbed her by the ass and pulled her close, her scent drew him in and he felt her shiver, "are you nervous?"

"Well, a little bit, of course," she laid her head on his shoulder, "it's different than just being online and chatting," She looked up at him with those big, blue eyes, "now it's real."

He touched her chin and reassured her, "you don't have to do anything you don't want, remember?"

"I know," she didn't sound as if she were so sure and he wondered when they were in the car driving to the appointed meeting place if either of them were.

They took two seats at the bar and ordered cocktails; both of them sucked down their first drink quickly and started a second before they seemed to be relaxed enough to speak. A man entered the bar and stood near the door, looking at face, "I wonder if that's him," Susan leaned closer and whispered.

"I hope not," Anthony spoke quietly, their foreheads almost touching, "he's definitely not in good shape," the man's gut was even bigger than his own.

Susan giggled, "No definitely not," she took another gulp and gestured with her head, "what about that guy?"

A young, blond man made his way down the aisle to a chair; he was fit and trim but looked as if he were still underage, "no way," Anthony said, "he's way too young."

"He's a baby," Susan agreed and once they started their third cocktails the comments kept coming and they held hands, knees touching and Anthony felt his cock knocking for attention, she looked far too lovely to resist and they were at a hotel.

He looked at the time and wondered if the mystery man wasn't going to be a no-show, "hey, baby, would you rather just go up to the room? Just you and me?" he felt sentimental and it showed.

"Sure," she shrugged her shoulders and smiled, "you know I am good with just you, right Anthony?"

Before he could answer, he felt the grip of the hand on his shoulder and it all came crystal clear. "Tony, small world, isn't it?" there was only one person who called him that and he looked up to see the tall man who was clenching his shoulder and towered over him look to his right to stare openly at Susan, "this is the lovely wife?"

Susan puckered her full, lower lip when she smiled at him and offered her hand, "hi, I'm Susan, how are you?"

Charles let go of Anthony's shoulder to take her hand in both of his and bend his head to press his lips to her palm, "you are breathtaking," he told her before releasing her from his grasp.

"What are you doing here?" Anthony couldn't wait for him to leave.

"Damnedest thing," his boss had bent his head to speak amongst the three of them but Anthony noticed that he was staring down Susan's dress the whole time, "I do a little swinging and so I was looking for a couple to play with," Anthony felt the trickle of sweat run down his neck, "and I met this hot blond online," he squinted as if it were all suddenly revealed. "Wait," his hand was wrapped around Susan's forearm now, "are you the couple looking for a third?"

"Oh my God!" Susan squealed and Anthony watched as she batted her eyelashes at him suggestively and the breath left him, "it's you! Anthony, how weird is that?" she asked him, "sit down," she said to Charles, patting the seat next to her.

"Well, this is my lucky night," Charles said, taking the seat next to her and pulling it even closer. Anthony couldn't hear the words of the conversation anymore because he was drawn to the man's hand, now planted on Susan's thigh. "You, my dear, are even more delicious in person than you were in your video," Anthony recalled her words from the other night. The man claimed to have an enormous cock that she would need to train for, his stomach churned at the recollection.

"Thank you," Susan's attentions were strictly on him now, her hand on his forearm as she spoke in her soft, little girl voice, "I can hardly wait to see what you've got for me."

"That is mutual," Charles stared at her cleavage and Anthony watched as his boss took her hand off his forearm and placed it under the bar, on the crotch of his pants, which Anthony could see, sported an impressive bulge, "I'm ready if you are."

"My God, you are ready!" Susan kept her hand on him long after he placed her there and Anthony watched her run her small fingers up and down his erection that strained to get at her, "are you ready?" she turned to Anthony as an afterthought.

It was a dizzying mix, the words and the images all culminating at once and Anthony was flushed and sweating, turned on and angry, jealous and leaking in his pants all at the same time. He looked at her, Susan's blond hair almost touching his boss' face, watching her take his cock would be exquisite torture, he stood up as if his body had made the decision for him, "sure, let's do this."

The three of them made their way to the room that Anthony had booked, Susan in the middle, her arms linked in both of theirs but her smiles and giggles were all for Charles. When

Anthony opened the door, he watched her walk past, the tiny dress had ridden up and her cheeks were barely concealed. Susan walked to the bed alone and sat, looking at one and then the other, cooing, "Come here boys."

Charles rushed past him and eagerly pushed her down on the bed, his mouth on hers, smearing her pink lipstick with fast, hungry kisses that turned into bites, "I came so fucking hard watching you masturbate in that schoolgirl outfit," he spoke slowly between ravishing Anthony's wife, pushing her dress up to her waist as he straddled her and then Anthony saw his boss' hand wander down between her legs.

"God, you're soaking wet," Charles made his way down to the floor and moaned as he approached her thighs, his tongue darting out to trace a line over her damp fabric from her opening to her mound, "is that what you need?" he asked her.

Anthony watched Susan shiver under his touch and gasp, "yes, please," and his wife moved her hips against the bed and stared at the man who was about to slide the tiny, black G-string down her legs.

Anthony listened to his heart pound but his hand touched his zipper and rubbed as his boss held his tongue out over Susan's swollen, bare lower lips and then with one touch, found his wife's pink clitoris and he heard her sigh as she pushed up for more, "you taste so good," Charles told her before lapping at her again, slowly teasing her just the way Anthony knew she liked it.

"Yes, oh that feels so good," she whimpered and Anthony saw her hands clutch the bed below as if she needed to hold on to something, the pleasure was so overwhelming. Anthony unzipped and freed his throbbing dick as his eyes took in the sight of her taking her pleasure.

"That's what you need, Susan," Charles' voice was muffled, his face pressed up against his wife's dripping cunt, but Anthony heard every word, "you need a man to lick that sweet pussy of yours, don't you?"

"Oh, yeah, I need that so bad," Anthony gritted his teeth and started working his hand up and down on his dick.

"A real man, to make you cum in his mouth, like your bitch husband doesn't do, is that right, Susan?" it was almost as if Charles knew the words that they spoke to each other in the bed and Anthony bit one hand hard while the other stroked even faster.

"Yes, I need a real man, one that can fuck me hard after I cum all over his face," she was moaning and thrashing under the tongue that had brought her to the edge of the first orgasm she would have with another man.

"That's good, because I have a big, hard dick to give you," Charles sounded like an animal as he growled at her and Anthony watched as he started to unbuckle with his tongue still tracing the ridge around his wife's bud.

Anthony held his erection hard at the base, his cock jolting in his hand, spitting his clear, salty liquid, it ran down his shaft and he told himself he couldn't cum yet no matter how desperately he wanted to.

Charles rose from his knees to finish taking down the pants and pulled his shirt off over his head as well. When he was naked, Anthony heard Susan whisper, "oh my God, you're so handsome," and he knew that there was a puddle of her desire under her and that the river of her juices was running from between her legs as she ran her eyes over the man's frame. Hell, Anthony hated him and still couldn't take his eyes off the broad, flexed shoulders, his firm, rounded pecks, his sculpted abs, the square, solid thighs, but his erection stopped him from looking anywhere else.

His boss had a long, thick cock, rock hard and beckoning to Susan, as if telling her to give in and take it all. Anthony watched Susan rise to a sitting position, and he watched his wife part her lips and run her tongue along the solid, wet tip of the man's dick.

Something snapped inside and Anthony stopped her, "Susan, wait," it had been the first time that either of them had looked away from each other and he watched as his wife turned her head, tongue out, eyes hazy from want, "I changed my mind."

"I thought this was what you wanted," she withdrew her tongue but her eyes were still on Charles.

"Yeah, what the fuck, Tony?" the taller, stronger man was clearly in charge in the room as he was at the office.

"I'm sorry," Anthony murmured, his face was hot with his shame and his cock was aching with want, his body rebelled against his words, "I just changed my mind."

Charles got dressed quickly, "that's OK, I understand, not a lot of husbands can really watch their wives get fucked well for once," the comment burned but he finished dressing, bent down to press his lips on Susan's briefly, leaving her sighing at his touch, "you should call me if you change your mind, beautiful."

The door shut behind him and before Anthony even heard the click, he was on the bed, pants down, taking his rightful place on top of her, kissing her hard, her tongue in his mouth as he sucked it into him and the head of his dick pressed against her heat, "you are so wet, baby," he panted.

"I know," she moved under him, sighing, "I need you inside me now," her hands were on his ass and she pressed her feet there as well to push him inside.

Anthony plunged into her, filling her to the bottom in one fast movement and rocking in and out of her, his wife covering his dick with her stream of desire, the wet noises of their coupling grew louder with every thrust, his balls were full and slapped against her lips. His eyes were on hers and he found that despite what had just happened, the words came back to him quickly, "you loved that big cock in your mouth, didn't you?" his body shook as he continued pushing in and pulling out.

"Yes," Susan panted and the look on her eyes said everything, "he's so fucking sexy, and that dick," she was squeezing him inside, he wondered if she could cum just talking about him, "it was the biggest cock I've ever seen."

"And you loved it in your mouth," Anthony wheezed, on the

verge of filling her with every last drop of his orgasm, he could feel his dick tense, "you looked like such a whore with your tongue out for him."

"Yes, fuck me like a whore, do it," she held onto him tightly and the roll of her release pulled him inside as she clenched and her hips trembled with the wave of her want.

"Yes, I'm cumming, baby," he unloaded with his cock buried inside, her wet walls grabbing him and milking his cock, sucking the release out of him with a roar as he continued to push and grind and empty himself inside his beautiful wife.

It was the first of the three times that they would make love that night and although he spoke about the man who had been in the bed with her each time, he could never bring himself to say his name.

Anthony was finishing up the last of the presentation and looking it over carefully, knowing that Charles would study it for mistakes, he was determined that it would be perfect. Over the last week, he had been driven at work. Something was different about his performance and only the two of them knew what it was but Anthony was determined to win.

"Tony, glad I caught you," his boss stuck his head in through the door without knocking at all, a new habit that Anthony had noticed recently, "I've got some more revisions for you," the man tossed a stack of papers on his desk and Anthony knew the smile on his face was a grimace. "You doing OK?" he asked, as if he could tell what the expression meant.

"Fine, sir," Anthony was bubbling over inside, every time he looked at the man now, he remembered him on top of Susan, standing, the meaty dick that his wife wanted so badly, it was a constant mix of pornographic pictures in his head and wanting to choke him, "just want to get this done so I can get home to the wife."

"God, that's right, Susan," Charles acted as if he didn't remember every single detail as well, "how's she doing?"

"She's good," Anthony nodded his head and refused to elaborate.

"Well, give her my best," Charles headed to the door and added, "oh, that's right, you can't," he snickered before adding, "I'm off, have a good night."

Anthony clenched his fists and listened to the pulse roar in his ears. He had to stop, he'd give himself a heart attack and he took a deep breath and closed his eyes. The problem was, it was still so fucking sexy, he couldn't help but want it, even if it was Charles. He could see her clearly, on the bed, dress up to her waist, panties down around her ankles over the black heels and the man between her legs making her moan. Anthony's dick sprang to life, he had been hard most of the time since that day, no amount of masturbating made it go away and he had fucked Susan like a new man every night.

Had he made a huge mistake by not letting Charles have her? Is that why it had permeated his brain in some way that he couldn't reverse? Her pink tongue, flicking out to lick up his precum, she had been drenched when Anthony touched her, so perfectly hot, the man had brought her almost to the edge with his words and the tip of his tongue.

He fought to keep his mind on his work, the longer he sat here daydreaming about it, the longer it would take for him to get home to her. It was dark outside when he noticed the flash at the bottom of his screen. It was Susan on instant messenger, something she never did when he was at work. He clicked the button and stared at the screen.

Her voice called to him, "Anthony, baby, can you see me?" she was on the web cam and he could see every inch. She had the pigtails in her hair again and the slutty schoolgirl outfit on, she waved to the camera and wiggled her hips, the breathy giggle made him tremble with want. "Hi, baby, you can see me, right?"

"Yes, Susan, what are you doing?" he looked around, knowing that no one else was there to hear, "you look so hot."

"You think?" she bent down a bit so that her cleavage was in view and he moaned, her beautiful tits just there for the touching and he was stuck here in his chair. "What about this?" she turned around and bent over so that her white string that ran up her crack was in view, she peaked around her shoulder, "you like that, Anthony?"

His pants were unzipped and his cock was out at his desk, he couldn't help it, the outfit drove him crazy and she knew this would be his response, "you know I like it," he whimpered as he started to touch himself for her.

"You know who else likes it?" she asked in her sing-song way.

"Who?" a thick droplet of liquid ran from his slit, down his shaft and puddled on his balls as he felt his thighs clench.

"Hello, Tony, how are you?" his boss' face appeared in the camera and his smile was wicked, "getting a lot of work done I see."

"Fuck, what are you doing there?" Anthony groaned, his fantasy was quickly turning into his nightmare.

"You can see what I'm doing here," Charles grabbed Susan from behind by the hips, he was naked and that enormous dick was rubbing up against his wife's behind, "in fact, we're going to let you watch the whole thing."

Her little, white panties that Anthony lusted after were torn off, like the slutty schoolgirl she was. Susan moaned and arched her back when the dick touched her bare flesh. "God, yes, give me your cock, I can't stop thinking about it," she begged his boss, "I need a real man's dick so bad."

Anthony watched as the man plunged inside and his wife howled, "Yes, take my pussy, fill it up, I love the way you feel inside me."

She slapped her bottom against him and Anthony couldn't tear his eyes away as his wife was filled with the enormous root, back and forth, thrusting into his wife so hard that she was up on her tip-toes. Anthony was shaking; his cock jolted and his hand gripped himself even tighter as he watched her take it all.

His boss threw his head back as he rocked her back and forth and told her, "you have the juiciest, little pussy, I'm going to fill you with so much cum your husband will be tasting me inside you for days."

The words made Anthony explode, he felt his orgasm rip from him and his whole body came in hard, pounding pulses, he watched the torrent of cum shoot from his dick, all over his hand, the desk, the screen, he let out a sound of pure lust as he coated himself with his ejaculation.

The lovers on camera had reached their own orgasms, separate from his and now Charles pulled her hair as he pushed every last drop of his sticky mess deep inside her shuddering cunt, his perfect ass flexing with every move. When he was done, he patted her bottom, "go show him what he has to look forward to."

Watching her obey him was the worst, Susan did as she was told and walked quickly to the camera, propping one leg up on the bed so that she could show him the gobs of cream that his boss had left behind. "Tony, can you hear me?" Charles was out of view but still completely in command.

"Yes, sir," Anthony knew that he'd have to call him sir forever now.

"When you come home, I want you to lick her clean, suck all of my cum out of your dirty, little bitch, do you understand me?" he demanded.

Anthony saw that it was far too late to turn back the fantasy now and knew his new lot, "yes, sir," he whispered.

"You really are a great employee," Charles added before hanging up on him.

BOOK 4: AFRAID TO LOSE HIM

She was simply and totally in love with him and that was the problem. Daphne had known somehow that it was impossible from the beginning and she'd tried to stop, like an addict, she'd ration him out, day by day, hour by hour, but like an addict, she could never get enough. He had rapidly become her obsession and then, yesterday, it all came tumbling down.

Daphne had almost decided that not knowing would be better, but it was too late, she was being punished for her snooping and it was a far worse fate than she deserved. The website address had popped up automatically in his browser, the site remembered his login and password, technically all she did was click here and there. She wished she would have paid attention to the sick churning in her stomach that told her to leave well enough alone.

Yet there was the picture, Daniel's handsome face was smiling back at her, his dark, curly hair, his vivid, blue eyes that she frequently found herself lost in, the one dimple that she couldn't stop kissing, the smile that he flashed at her in the morning over coffee, it was him and yet it wasn't the man she knew at all. A virtual stranger with the same name was advertising his secret predilections here and she couldn't help but gasp as she read.

Was it better that he only cheated on her with other men? He had told her that she was the one, specifically he had said, "You're the only woman I want to kiss," and at the time, her heart had melted as the rest of her had in his arms. Now she wondered if it hadn't all been an easy out.

His ad read like a hard-core porn movie, he was available to "hook up" with men, he was a "bottom" and liked big cocks, the bigger and blacker, the better. He liked it rough, he wanted their abuse and every time she read the words to herself, she pictured him on his knees somewhere in the dark and her heart broke a little more.

She ignored his phone calls that day as she fumed and fidgeted, smoking one cigarette after another, the ashtray was overflowing and she was still no closer to an answer. Daphne tried to close her eyes and clear her mind and all she could see was Daniel over her, in the bed, his mouth on hers, his hands roaming her body in the seductive caress that had been her undoing since the first night they had spent together.

She moaned and felt the flutter between her legs. Deprived of his touch and his kisses and his naked body in this self-imposed exile, she ached for him and slid two fingers down the front of her pants and into the wet panties underneath, she was soaked and her clitoris thudded impatiently for attention. Daniel would lay between her legs with his face buried there for an hour, slowly and carefully bringing her to her first, tumultuous orgasm, followed by a course of peaks and valleys, again and again she would find herself shuddering under his embrace.

She needed him and as she continued to work her fingers in the circular motion that brought her closer and closer to her release, her sighs became louder and the picture of him there, naked and worshiping every dripping inch of her pink crevice, was more vivid.

As she reached her crescendo, suddenly another face was there. Another man, behind her lover, she couldn't see what he was doing, but she knew. Of course she did, the low, raspy noises that came from him, lost in his own pleasure, Daniel had a lover of his own.

Daphne came hard, suddenly waves raced through her body and her thighs trembled and her hips rocked back and forth and she felt the rivulet of her want running from her opening the bed below. Crying as she continued to tumble through it, her climax was intense and continued even after she had removed her hand and only held her thighs together, letting the sensation flood her.

Afterward, she realized that she had an answer, but it wasn't what she had expected.

They had a lovely dinner and she only felt a twinge of guilt when she lied about her unreturned phone calls for a moment, instead she held his hand to her lips and kissed his palm, his was the greater sin and she wasn't sure if she were about to give absolution or take him down with her.

He was already kissing her when he walked through the door and his hands had worked down from the small of her back to cup the cheeks of her ass and pull her by the hips to grind his hard cock against her, "God, I missed you Daphne, I want you so much, honey," Daniel whispered in her ear and his breath on her neck was gently undoing her plan.

"I want to try something," she forced herself to stop, she had come this far, she wouldn't throw it all away just because he was making her nipples hard and her breath come faster and harder from his scent and his touch. "Just play along, OK?" she asked.

"Oh, kinky," he raised his eyebrows and smiled lasciviously at her and Daphne wondered if he'd feel the same way in a few moments.

She turned on the TV and hit play on the DVD. She had watched the movie from beginning to end and had paused it at the point she thought would be most intriguing. The couple on the bed were naked, her long, blond curls were strewn across the white pillow beneath her and a sheen of sweat shone on her face, her mouth was open and her sighs came faster as the handsome man on top of her moved down her body.

Daniel sat next to her on the couch, obviously surprised but riveted by the porn, "Wow, what's gotten into you?" he touched her knee as he sat, drawn in as he watched the blond on the screen in ecstasy.

"Keep watching," Daphne told him, her hand moving slowly up his inner thigh to his thick cock, he was even harder than he'd been at the door and she felt the beginning of a wet spot in the crotch of his pants.

The man on the screen, dark-haired, buff, tan and perfect, had the biggest dick that Daphne had ever seen and as he raised up on his knees, it came into full view, the head of his long, engorged dick was coated with precum that dripped from him onto the blonde's belly. Daphne noticed that the erection in her hand throbbed at the sight of him. She slowly unbuckled and unzipped him, Daniel's underwear was soaked and she started running the palm of her hand back and forth slowly along his shaft.

"Daphne, what are you doing to me?" he whispered to her but never took his eyes off the screen and watched the beautiful man as he kissed the blonde's belly, licking up the hot, juices that had spilled there. Daniel moaned and she knew it was time to take him to the next step.

"Get down on the floor, Daniel," it wasn't a request and perhaps he heard that it was more of a command, although perhaps it was that he was so lost in the images in front of him that he was that malleable, either way, Daniel dropped to his knees on the rug.

Daphne slid the pants off the bottom of his legs and then the underwear, he moved as directed, his eyes drilled to the screen and he never questioned what she was doing behind him. As the man on the screen arrived between the blonde's legs and his tongue started to caress her there, the camera panned to the door and a tall, naked black man entered the room and went straight to the bed to join the couple.

She heard Daniel gasp and her fingers made slow circles around the tender skin on his cheeks as he watched the black man do the same to the stud on the bed. Daphne followed the black lover's lead and bent her head to Daniel's crack and kissed his puckered, pink skin around his anus. She felt his thighs tremble and his thrust as his body responded to her caress and she noticed the material of her panties was soaked through as she watched him.

Her tongue darted out and tasted him, sliding inside his pink bud and his cry of pleasure shocked her, it was hot and urgent and he moved his hips back and forth to give her all of it as he watched the black man take the man in the same way. The black lover's pink tongue had pushed inside the man and lapped back and forth the same way the man was licking the blond. Daniel was enraptured and never stopped her, even when her tongue became her wet finger, if anything every inch of him screamed for more.

Daphne worked her finger inside, steadily penetrating her lover and once she felt the small indentation there, she beckoned up and down and felt Daniel's ass tighten around her as he roared and pleaded with her, "yes," again and again. She fucked him harder then, sliding her finger in and out and continuing to pulse the tip of it on his prostate when she filled him.

"Oh my God," Daniel had his hand on his cock and started jerking himself up and down to the tempo of her finger, he watched the screen and she found her ecstasy welling up inside as she watched him, knowing she controlled him now, a power she had never felt before ran through her body like an electric current and she decided that she would push him yet again.

The vibrator was in the drawer close by and he whimpered when she withdrew her touch, only to cry out to her when she slid the well-lubricated toy in its place. It was the perfect moment, the black man, his beefy cock that looked well-oiled and dripped with its need for the lover was stroking up and down the man's crack, pushing against his hole, teasing him. The man threw his head back with a howl and backed his bottom up to meet the black man's stiff pole, "yes, fuck me, do it, fuck that ass," he was panting and more than ready and the black man eased his way in and now rocked in and out of the lover the same way Daphne moved the toy back and forth inside Daniel.

Daniel was teetering on the edge of his orgasm and when she touched his throbbing spot inside, he clutched his cock even harder, his whole body quivering as he came in a long, hot spurt that spilled from his hand and shot up to his chest and burst from him over and over until he collapsed on the floor. Daphne gently withdrew her toy and kissed his cheek salaciously before resting on her heels, pressing the stop button on the remote and waiting for him to make the next move.

"Come here," his voice was quiet; he had rolled to his side and opened his arms for her to join him. She did as he asked and stared into his eyes, the picture of him online staring back at her. "Where did you learn that?" he glowed, there was no way for him to deny that he had loved every minute.

"Nowhere, just something I was thinking of," she murmured and opened her lips to accept his tongue inside, he could taste himself in her mouth and she found him sucking on the tip of her tongue, as if not wanting to waste it. When he released her, she asked, "Did you like it?" knowing the answer, waiting for a confession.

"Yes, I loved it," his lips were on her neck and nibbled her earlobe and she wondered if he couldn't look her in the eye when he lied, whispering, "I've never done anything like that before."

Daphne bit her lip, if she were ever going to admit what she knew, it was now. Instead, she kissed him passionately and let him pick her up and carry her to the bedroom where he made love to her well into the night.

Two days later, the rosy haze of orgasms had faded and Daphne found herself spying on him again. She hated the thought and her cheeks burned with shame as she clicked and clicked, but it didn't stop her, worse, it seemed to propel her further.

This morning, there were two new pictures on his profile and she held her breath as she opened the first one. No one would know it was him if they hadn't seen him, as she had, and memorized every line of his naked body with her fingers. One picture was of his penis, only half-erect, it lay to the side, pink and slick with his sweet, salty liquid, the second was him on his knees, only his ass and the back of his thighs.

She found herself shaking her head no, her heart thudding in her chest as she read the updated information. Her love was available to give blow jobs at any time, a quick comparison made him sound like a common street corner whore. Daphne grabbed her cell phone and her finger hovered over his name, all she had to do was punch it and let him know that the charade was up.

Always stubborn, she decided that since she was already a spy and a liar, she would take another step down in her demise and quickly clicked some more. She was almost afraid of what she had just done, but there it was, her own profile, a fake picture and a new email account that she had just set-up, Daphne decided that if she was going to play the game, she'd play to win.

Her gay alter-ego sent her lover a carefully worded message so that none of Daphne would shine through, only Jason, the young, black man whose rippled abs were on display for Daniel to drool over, would speak for her.

"Hey, Saw your profile, are you 4 reel?" she hit send before she could talk herself out of it.

A reply came back to her within minutes, sent from Daniel's phone, and her pulse throbbed in her throat so loudly it was all she could hear. "You are gorgeous and yes I am real. You've seen my pics, would love to see your big, black dick before I suck it."

Daphne was quick to find an acceptable photo and in minutes, had crafted her message, "You think you can handle this?" Jason asked Daniel.

He must have been waiting for the picture because the response was almost instantaneous. "I can't wait to try. So fucking hard looking at your cock. Thinking about you shoving it down my throat and feeding me your cum."

Her shame was gone, it was something else entirely and when she quickly wrote her response, she couldn't have explained it to him, or anyone else. "You gonna suck my big cock first and then I want that nice, white ass."

Daniel wrote back quickly and begged for the opportunity, "Please pound my ass, all I want is to be your little cock whore."

Daphne realized at that moment what it was, pulling at her, egging her on, it was the same dark shadow that had reared up when she had touched herself the other day, desire. Suddenly the thought of watching Daniel split open by the huge, dark erection was something that wouldn't go away.

"I'm gonna make you my whore, little white bitch. And when I'm done, I'm pissing all over you too so you never forget who is your Master."

Daniel's question was a checkmate, "Where and when Master?"

She strummed her fingers, the scenarios popping up one by one and each quickly discarded. She didn't know if the challenge was turning her on almost as much as the daydream images in her mind, but she rose to meet it, check and mate. "Your house, tonight, slave."

Several minutes passed, Daniel hadn't responded and she almost thought she had succeeded in calling his bluff when the message came. "Can't be my house, on the DL, but I will get a motel for us." She had to search "DL" on the computer to learn what it meant and she didn't know if she could keep herself from calling him after all.

The idea hit her, a sickening combination of salacious and scary, she didn't know if she really had the courage to do it, but she had gone this far.

The next afternoon, she called Daniel at work, and asked him in a low purr, "What are you doing tonight, honey?"

"Oh honey," he sighed, as if frustrated, "I've got to stay late, my boss is on my ass about the sales numbers again."

His lie was one more piece of the puzzle in place and she couldn't help but smirk to herself at the irony of Daniel's use of, "on my ass". He was so close and still, he had no idea what awaited for him. Half delirious with her X-rated frame by frame movie that slipped through her imagination, half choking with rage, she still didn't know which would win when she saw his face later.

"Well I'll miss you Daniel," she murmured and added, "I'll be thinking hot thoughts about you." She could hardly hold back her laugh, pressing her lips together to keep it inside, just a little while longer.

"Daphne, you know I'll be thinking about you too, baby," and told her he loved her before hanging up. The question was, was it all a lie?

The hotel was out of the way, on a dead end street and the parking lot was dark. It seemed to be specifically designed for illicit trysts and she had picked it for that reason. Parked in the corner, she had the advantage, hunkered down in the front seat, she could see him enter and park and he never looked in her direction.

She got the call that she had been expecting and quickly confirmed the details. When she hung up, she watched as the next man parked and made his way inside. The final play was about to be made and she checked her lipstick and her hair quickly in the rear view, she wanted to be stunning.

Daphne went to the front desk and smiled, the young man behind the counter would be an easy pawn. "Hi, how are you? I was wondering if you can do me a favor?" she batted her eyelashes and wiggled her shoulders in the low-cut sweater that hugged her voluptuous curves. "I'm such an airhead, my husband gave me the key to our room and I guess I lost it already. Can you give me another one?"

"Sure, ma'am," the boy was staring at her cleavage and never made eye contact, only asking, "what room?"

"It's 302. You're a doll," she kept the game going until she had the card in her hand, waving at him as she flipped her hair back, "thanks!" It was all coming together so well.

She almost ran down the hall to the door, but when she stopped there at 302, she felt the panic wash over her in a wave. Was she really ready for this? She tilted her ear to the door, she heard nothing and slowly, quietly, she slid the card in the slot and opened the door, quickly closing it behind her. The only sound was the shower running in the background.

The tall, dark man on the bed was only wearing underwear, and Daphne sighed as her eyes roamed his body up and down. His skin gleamed in the low light and every line flexed with muscle and his wide chest seemed to melt into the smaller, rippled lines around his waist and then her gaze stopped at his crotch. She had seen what was barely able to hide there, under the tight fabric; the cock bulged out of the top of his underwear even when at half-mast. Her exhale was long and the goose bumps raced up her back.

She walked toward him, heels silent in the carpet, she started unbuttoning the sweater that had gained her entry, and she smiled when the man's eyes caressed her slowly, waiting for her to slide down the shorts and show him every tasty inch.

Daphne sat close to him, wearing only the black bra and matching thong, their thighs touched and she let her hand finally reach out and stroke the solid shoulder, then the flexed curve of his bicep and run down his smooth, chocolate skin to his sculpted abs. She was just about to slip her hand under the waistband of his underwear when the bathroom door opened.

"Hello, Daniel," she purred, just as she reached inside to touch the huge erection that waited for her.

"What!" he backed up slowly, his mouth open, his hard-on melting in front of her eyes, "Oh God," he shook his head no and all she could do was smile.

"Surprise!" Daphne laughed, she couldn't help the little bit of evil bubbling up inside, the satisfaction of knowing that she'd caught him at his own game, but there it was again, the problem, she loved him. "Come here," she crooked her finger at him and patted the mattress, her hand on another man's dick, she watched him shuffle to the bed and sit down gingerly, as if terrified to even be near her.

"I am Jason," she finally confessed and she watched his expression change from fear to anger to embarrassment.

His face was in his hands as he choked out the words, "I never actually did this before. I only talked and thought about it, I never met anyone," he couldn't look at her when he lied though.

Daphne tugged on his chin and forced his eyes up to meet her, "Well, then I hope you like your initiation, Daniel. Because your fantasy is about to become fulfilled," and her hand grabbed the huge cock tighter as she added, "and so is mine."

She turned away from her lover and melted onto the bed with the black man, pulling his underwear down to finally free the thick, black pole inside, she opened her mouth and felt his hot tongue explore her. Their kiss was hard and wet and she sucked his tongue and shivered as she imagined his mouth all over her body. "Daniel," she reached out to touch his arm, too busy to look at him, "you know what you need to do, honey."

"What?" he whispered.

"Get down there and suck that big, black dick. Remember? You want him to feed it to you, inch by inch, down your throat, right?" she could almost quote him word for word and she wanted to watch him fulfill every promise.

"Please, Daphne," he moved to the floor and was on his knees, a supplicant, throwing himself on her mercy, "I never did this, I don't know if I can."

"Oh no," she sighed, the black lover was kissing her neck now and pulling the bra down to her shoulder, "you'll do as you're told. You're the little whore, the slave, right Daniel?" her tone was like glass and she could see his shoulders slump in resignation.

She watched as he finished removing the man's underwear, slipping them off his feet and opened his mouth, Daniel's lips parted and his tongue out to lick the head of the dripping dick. She looked to the man beside her as he whispered, "yes, suck that big cock," and she shivered as Daniel complied.

The man beside her unhooked her bra and his strong fingers pulled on one nipple as the wet, slurping noises continued. Daniel's wet mouth rocked up and down on the man's engorged erection, only half of the penis was inside and she could see that his cheeks were puffed out and it was a struggle for him to continue. Although she was enjoying every minute of it, she remembered that he had begged for abuse and decided to dish it out, she pushed his head down on the dick and heard Daniel gag, "suck on that dick, you fucking whore. I want to see your lips down to his big balls."

The man traded his fingers for his lips and in a moment, Daphne laid back on her elbows, moaning as his wide tongue grazed and his teeth softly nibbled her pink point as she continued to direct Daniel. "Harder, come on Daniel, show that black cock the respect it deserves," and the muffled sound that came from Daniel meant he was finally ready to give in. She watched his head bob up and down faster now, showing her what a good whore he could be.

"That's it, honey," she could barely speak, the fluttering between her legs and the sweet sensation on her nipple, she was soaking wet and needed more. The man beside her groaned and pulled his erection from Daniel's mouth, he knew the plan and was under strict instructions.

"Come here, baby," she cooed and looked into Daniel's eyes as he made his way up to the bed, she smiled and cocked her head, answering the question that was there, the one that she had obsessed over every step of the game. "I love you, Daniel," she reached up to touch his face and felt him crumble in her arms.

Kissing her desperately, he pressed his lips to every bit of her face, her neck, down to her breasts, "I'm so hard, God, Daphne I am so hot, watching you with him," he rubbed himself back and forth between her legs and started where the black lover had stopped, with his tongue lapping on first one hard nipple and then the next.

"Now you know how I feel," she tilted her hips up to accept his cock and shivered when he thrust inside, "I can't wait to watch you with him," the surprise wasn't over and she had kept the best for last.

She looked up and saw the black lover behind Daniel, mounting him, his large frame was so much wider than her love and the man bent and spit, a long line of saliva sliding down his crease and Daniel looked at her with a gasp, panic and want and shame and desire all there, so close to the surface. When the man entered him, he thrust inside Daphne with a low moan.

"God, yes, fuck me Daniel, fuck me like he fucks you," she was mesmerized and couldn't tear her eyes off the man behind her lover. She could hear the wet slap of skin on skin and knew that the bull's heavy ball sack was pushing against Daniel's thighs with every thrust, going deeper and deeper inside, opening him up wide like the whore he wanted to be.

"Daphne," he panted above her, sweat dripping off his forehead onto her naked body, his eyes were wild and he whimpered like a bitch the more cock he took, "God, he's so deep inside me!"

"That's right, Daniel," she was fluttering inside and she could feel her orgasm approaching, "you're going to love being my little whore. Taking all the cock I tell you to take, aren't you?" the thought of it was pushing her to the edge, controlling him like this, pimping him out and watching him beg for it was excruciatingly sweet.

She grabbed his chest, her release flooding his dick and holding him tight, her thighs shuddering as she came, "Daniel, fuck me harder, I'm cumming," and she clenched and released, pulling him in and coating him with her gush of sweet, sticky cum. She felt Daniel tense as he buried himself in her silky, wet pussy and she listened to him cry out for more.

"Daphne, he's cumming in me," Daniel threw his head back and she heard the black man let out a low growl as he spurt deep inside Daniel's stretched hole, the man was pounding quickly in and out as he came and the wet strokes got louder and louder the more of his hot, salty load he pushed inside.

"Take all that cum, little whore," she murmured and her words were too much for him, Daniel was shaking, every inch of his body was trembling as he finally let go and let his orgasm rock his body from head to toe.

When he collapsed on top of her, shivering and holding her close, she kissed his head and felt all of the bitterness seep out of her. She might share his body, but Daphne had his heart and that was all that mattered. One look, one touch and she knew that to be true.

After the black man had left, it was just the two of them and Daniel asked, "Can you forgive me?"

"Yes, I have," she nodded, but she couldn't help but smile mischievously and add, "however, things are going to be a little bit different from now on."

"Yes, how so?" he looked concerned.

"I'm in charge of you, little whore," her Mistress voice came back and she watched his eyes widen as all the possible scenarios ran through his imagination. "So no more gay hook-up websites."

"Of course not," he whispered, embarrassed again.
She kissed his cheek and told him the rules, "You can have all the cock you like as long as you have permission," it was the one thing that she wouldn't budge on.

"Yes?" he was waiting for the condition, it sounded too good to be true.
"And I'm there," she added, pulling him close once more.

More Books by Howie Hayes

The Sissy Series: Taboo Erotica Volume 1
Book 1 - A Sissy's Secret Desire: The Mistress, the Master and the Obedient Slave
Book 2 - Caught in the Act: A Sissies Secret Exposed
Book 3 - A Sissy in Training: Shaved and Submissive
Book 4 - His Secret is Out: Blackmail Never Felt So Good

The Sissy Series: Taboo Erotica Volume 2
Book 1 - Be Careful What You Wish For: The Sissy Inside of Him
Book 2 - The Sissy Cop and the Suspect: A Tranny, Pimp and the Sissy Cop
Book 3 - I'm Not Gay: Naughty Pleasures
Book 4- Weekend Sissy: Obey Thy Mistress

www.ingramcontent.com/pod-product-compliance
Ingram Content Group UK Ltd.
Pitfield, Milton Keynes, MK11 3LW, UK
UKHW022219230426
12048UKWH00016BA/949